My Friend Maya Loves to Dance

By Cheryl Willis Hudson

Illustrated by Eric Velasquez

WASHINGTON COUNTY PUBLIC LIBRARY
205 Oak Hill Street
Abingdon, VA 24210

Abrams Books for Young Readers, New York

The illustrations in this book were made with oil paint on 300 lb. watercolor paper.

Library of Congress Cataloging-in-Publication Data

Hudson, Cheryl Willis.
My friend Maya loves to dance / by Cheryl Willis Hudson ;
illustrated by Eric Velasquez.
p. cm.
Summary: Maya loves to dance, leap, pirouette, and bow
in tutus and leotards or kente cloth and cowrie shells.
ISBN 978-0-8109-8328-1
[1. Stories in rhyme. 2. Dance—Fiction. 3. African
Americans—Fiction.] I. Velasquez, Eric, ill. II. Title.

PZ8.3.H856My 2009
[E]—dc22
2008024685

Text copyright © 2010 Cheryl Willis Hudson
Illustrations copyright © 2010 Eric Velasquez
Book design by Melissa Arnst

Published in 2010 by Abrams Books for Young Readers,
an imprint of ABRAMS. All rights reserved. No portion of
this book may be reproduced, stored in a retrieval system,
or transmitted in any form or by any means, mechanical,
electronic, photocopying, recording, or otherwise, without
written permission from the publisher.

Printed and bound in China
10 9 8 7 6 5 4 3 2 1

Abrams Books for Young Readers are available at special
discounts when purchased in quantity for premiums and
promotions as well as fundraising or educational use.
Special editions can also be created to specification. For
details, contact specialmarkets@abramsbooks.com or
the address below.

ABRAMS
THE ART OF BOOKS SINCE 1949
115 West 18th Street
New York, NY 10011
www.abramsbooks.com

For the students and staff of
Marie Wildey School of Dance—
keep dancing!

–C. W. H. and E. V.

My friend Maya loves to dance.

Wherever there is music,
Maya takes a stance.
She points her toes,
Then away she goes.
Dancing is fun.

Maya knows!

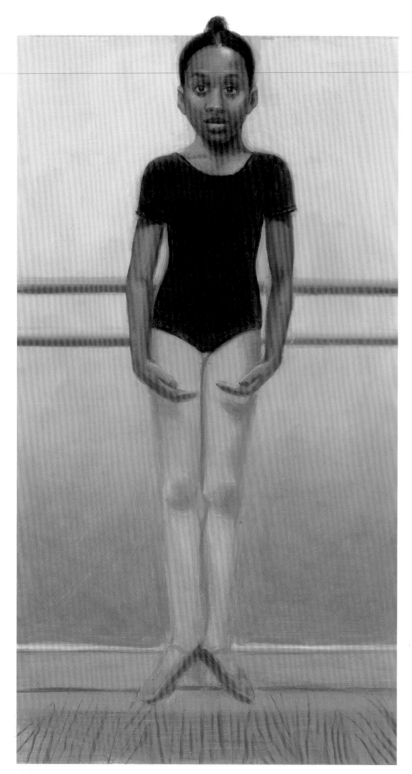

My friend Maya loves to leap.

She bends at the knees,

Never misses a beat.

She holds her arms high
To reach for the sky.

Jeté! Maya jumps. She's ready to fly!

My friend Maya
loves ballet class.

She stands near the *barre*
And looks straight at the glass.

Madame nods, "*Oui, oui,*
Grands pliés, ma jeune fille!"

"Très bien, très bien,
Mes amis!"

To jazz, blues, and rap.
She dances in the hall,
In church . . .

And at the mall.
When she's dancing,
Maya has a ball.

My friend Maya loves to dress
In leotards and tutus . . .

But kente cloth is best.
Dressed in cowrie shells or lace,
Maya dances with grace
And a look of pride on her face.

My friend Maya loves the sounds
Of cellos and trumpets
And drums all around.

She loves Bach and reggae
And to hear gospel play.
Music moves Maya
All through the day.

My friend Maya loves to plan
Pirouettes and bows,

And exits bold and grand.

She waits by the wall
For the next curtain call.
Dancing's fantastic.
Maya loves it all.

My friend Maya loves to dream
Of recitals and soft lights
And performing for a queen.
Maya dances strong and free
With joy all can see.

Dancing is magic
For her and for me.